Disclaimer

This is a work of fiction. Names, characters, organizations, spots, occasions and occurrences are either the results of the creator's creative energy or utilized as a part of an invented way. Any similarity to real people, living or dead, or genuine occasions is absolutely adventitious.

ISBN:
eBook: 978-1-946792-15-0
print:978-1-946792-16-7
audio/d :978-1-946792-17-4

© **2017 Urquhart Randolph**

Published by Glofton llc

Table of Contents

subscribe
VISIT US
Enroll in our VIP list.
Be the first to be notified on our latest published book.
Downloading for free gifts.

The Conference

Chapter 1 – A New Job

Kathryn took a deep breath and adjusted the front of her blouse. Having been a teacher for six years, she was surprised that she felt so nervous about orientation. The school was new and the students would be different, but she was passionate about teaching Language Arts. She couldn't wait to help a new batch of kids see just how exciting Literature could be.

Just get in there, she thought to herself. You do not want to start off the year by being late.

Kathryn opened the door of the library and felt her cheeks flush as twenty sets of eyes looked up at her. She smiled and quietly walked to an open seat at the closest table.

Once she was settled in, she began to look around at her colleagues. A group of older women sat together at a table in the corner. Kathryn could tell by watching their interactions that they had been teaching together for years.

She continued scanning the room and smiled as she spotted the three young faces of brand new teachers. Kathryn remembered how she felt when she got her first teaching assignment and made a mental note to approach the new ones and offer any help or support that they might need.

Next she looked over at the four male teachers sitting together. Three of them were dressed in professional attire, and she spent a bit of time trying to guess what subjects they taught. She figured that the oldest gentleman, with the grey hair and glasses, taught History. The youngest looked like he was a Math teacher, while the other may have taught Science.

She didn't need to spend much time wondering what the fourth man taught. He was wearing an athletic jacket with the word COACH embroidered on the back, had a whistle around his neck, and was flipping through a book on how to teach young people to properly stretch.

Man, she thought, shaking her head. I wonder if there is some sort of kit that guys need to buy before they let them teach PE at a school. They all seem to be the same.

Before she had a chance to look away, the PE teacher looked up from his book and made eye contact with her. She tried to look away from him, but found that there was something compelling about him. Although his clothing and posture were most definitely relaxed, there intensity in his dark brown eyes that she found intriguing.

The man gave her a slight smile, and Kathryn was alarmed to find her pulse quicken. She briefly nodded and looked away, silently vowing to avoid him for the rest of the day.

After a few minutes the rest of the staff had arrived and the Principal stepped to the front of the room to welcome everyone and begin the orientation. Kathryn enjoyed learning the policies and procedures for the school, and she was happy to get to meet her fellow Language Arts teachers. Before she knew it two hours had passed and it was time for their morning break.

Kathryn stood up and stretched, deciding to go outside and get some fresh air. As she turned to walk towards the door, she felt someone standing beside her. Before she even looked, she knew it was the PE teacher.

She slowly turned to face him and realized that he was much taller than she thought he was. She tilted her head up to see his face.

"Hello," he said, smiling down at her.

"Hello," she answered. "You're tall."

He laughed. "Yes, I am tall. I'm six feet, five inches to be exact. And you are not very tall."

Kathryn smiled. Despite her vow to avoid this gentleman, she was enjoying their interaction. "No, I'm not very tall. Five feet, two inches, to be exact."

"My name is Carson Hodges," he said, extending his hand. "Everyone calls me Hodge."

Kathryn shook his hand. "Hello, Hodge. It's nice to meet you. My name is Kathryn Nichols."

"Kathryn Nichols," Hodge repeated. "It's very nice to meet you."

Kathryn pulled her hand back and looked away. "Well, I'm going to go outside," she said, abruptly. "I want to take around and see more of the school. I'm sure I'll see you around."

Hodge blinked, then smiled. "See you around," he said.

Kathryn walked quickly walked outside. Stop it, right now, she thought. That's the last thing you need.

Sure, he's cute, but he's just like all the rest of them. Don't waste your time.

She shook her head, put the PE teacher out of her mind, and went about the task of exploring her new campus.

When she returned to the meeting she could tell that he was trying to get her attention, but she refused to look at him. Kathryn had already decided that Carson Hodges would mean nothing to her, and she was determined to prove it.

Chapter 2 – The First Day of School

"Jane Austen, Charles Dickens, The Bronte Sisters… these are just a few of the incredible authors that you are going to read over the course of the year," Kathryn said, smiling at her students. "Now, before you let those eye rolls turn into groans, hear me out."

The students chuckled.

"Here's the deal," Kathryn said, sitting on the edge of her desk. "I am not going to choose all of the books that you read. We are going to trade off – one for one. For every book that I assign, you get to choose a book on your own. It can be anything you want: wizards, vampires, space heroes... seriously. Whatever you want."

She sat back and watched as her students began to chatter excitedly with one another. A young lady in the back of the class raised her hand.

"Yes, Miss..." Kathryn looked down at her seating chart. "Jenkins," she finished, smiling at the girl.

"Are you serious? We actually get to read those types of books for school?"

Kathryn nodded. "Absolutely serious," she confirmed. "I figure that it is a great way to keep you motivated!"

The student nodded in agreement, and Kathryn let them talk to each other for a few more minutes before getting their attention once again.

"Okay, what we are going to do now is simply spend some time talking about books. What I need you to do is…" Her instructions were interrupted by the sound of the classroom door opening.

Everyone looked to see who would come in. When the visitor appeared, several of the girls in the room started to whisper.

"Hodge!" one of the students yelled out.

Hodge stepped all the way into the classroom and smiled.

"Hey, Rodgers," he responded to the student. He turned and looked at Kathryn. "Hello, Ms. Nichols. I am sorry to interrupt your class. I only need a minute, if that's okay."

Kathryn nodded. "That's fine, Mr. Hodges."

"Thank you," Hodge said. He then turned towards the students. "Well, as you all know, today is the first day of school, and this Friday night is the first home football game. I wanted to let you know that we will be having a pep rally Friday afternoon.

The band will be performing, the cheerleaders will be there, and there will be some fun games and prizes. After the rally, whoever comes to the game on Friday and wears our school colors will get in for free!"

The students cheered, and Hodge turned towards Kathryn.

"Oh, and Ms. Nichols, I know that this is your first year teaching here, and I'm not sure if you have any of our school gear yet. So, to make sure that you are taken care of and are truly ready to be part of our community, I have brought you your very own royal blue and white sweatshirt."

The students applauded as Hodge handed Kathryn the sweatshirt. "Thank you," she said, trying to fight the blush that was spreading across her cheeks. "I will wear it with pride."

Hodge smiled and turned to leave. "That's all I have," he said. "See you Friday!"

Once Hodge was gone, it took Kathryn several minutes to get her classroom back to order. The students were excitedly talking about the game, and she heard several girls gushing about how cute the football coach was.

One of the girls in the front row turned to Kathryn. "You're so lucky, Miss Nichols," she said.

"Why am I lucky?" Kathryn asked.

"Because Hodge gave you a sweatshirt. He is just gorgeous!"

Kathryn smiled. "He gave me a sweatshirt because I am new here, and he is the football coach. Luck has nothing to do with it!"

The girl giggled. "But don't you think he's gorgeous?"

Kathryn knew better than to answer that question. She simply replied, "That's what I've been told." The girls in the class giggled some more.

Kathryn tried to get everyone back on task, but she knew that she never really had their full attention.

Oh well, she thought. There's always tomorrow.

After school Kathryn sat in her room finalizing her lesson plans for the next day. She looked up at the sound of someone entering her room.

"It's me again," Hodge said, smiling. "I'm sorry to disturb you. Again."

Kathryn returned the smile, but tried not to appear too friendly. She didn't want his interruptions to become a frequent occurrence.

"I can see that you are busy," he said, motioning to the papers and books spread out on Kathryn's desk. "And I have to get back to practice. My assistants are running things right now; so let me get straight to the point. I was wondering if you would like to go and get a cup of coffee with me this evening."

Kathryn took a minute and looked down at her desk. Her first instinct was to accept the invitation. She found herself drawn to Hodge and wanted to get to know him more, but she knew she had to fight that impulse. Taking a deep breath, she looked up and forced herself to make eye contact with him.

"Thank you," she said, hoping that her voice sounded calmer than she felt. "I appreciate the invitation, and I am flattered. But I don't think it would be wise."

Hodge looked a bit surprised, but smiled kindly. "Well then, no problem. I will just see you around school."

Kathryn looked back down at her desk so she wouldn't be tempted to stop him from leaving.

Let him go, she thought. It's better this way. Don't you remember what happened with Mark?

She sighed and looked out the window, feeling thankful that she didn't have a view of the football field. She thought for a moment about Mark, the boy who had stolen her heart in college. She remembered his tall, athletic body. She remembered how much she enjoyed sitting in the stands and watching him play basketball, and how she would feel when he would wave at her from the court.

Then she remembered walking in on him and her roommate, seeing them locked in an embrace that was much more than friendly.

She remembered running from her apartment, tears streaming down her face, vowing to never go back.

Never again, she thought. Never again will I let an athlete break my heart.

Pleased with her decision to reject Hodge's offer, Kathryn forced all thoughts of men from her mind. She looked down at her notes and went back to her work with renewed energy.

Chapter 3 – A Very Special Student

"Okay, class, so tell me. Why do you think that Mr. Darcy was so quiet at the dance?"

Kathryn smiled as several hands shot up in the air. She was pleased to see that so many of her students were enjoying reading the classic literature.

School had only been in session for three weeks, but already they had finished a novel by Dickens, read one of their own choosing, and had now started on Austen. Although the customs and traditions of the past were very different, the themes of love and romance were very much relevant today.

Kathryn called on someone to begin the discussion, and sat back to observe while the debate raged on. As she looked around the room she couldn't help but notice that one of the students, Ryan Gregory, was not engaged at all in what was happening. He simply sat and stared out at the window, seemingly oblivious to all that was going on around him.

When the discussion was over Kathryn gave the students the next reading assignment and then went and sat at her desk. She was concerned about Ryan.

He had been the same way the day before, sitting and staring off into space. Up until then, though, he had been friendly and outgoing, eagerly participating in class. She decided that she would speak to him in private to see what was going on and if there was anything she could do to help.

When the bell rang to dismiss the students, Kathryn asked Ryan to come to her desk for a minute. He looked surprised by her request, but nodded his head in agreement.

"Yes, Miss Nichols?" he asked, fiddling with the straps of his backpack.

"Hey, Ryan," Kathryn said, kindly. "Are you okay? I noticed that today and yesterday you seemed a little bit out of it in class."

Ryan looked down at the floor. "Yeah, I'm fine," he said. "I guess I'm just a bit tired."

"Are you sure?" Kathryn asked. "That's all it is?"

Ryan nodded, still looking at the floor.

Kathryn sighed. "Okay," she said. "I just wanted to make sure. Just know that I'm here if anything ever comes up that you want talk about, okay?"

Ryan nodded again. "Thanks," he mumbled. He glanced over at the door.

"You can go," Kathryn said. "I don't want you to be late to your next class."

"Okay, see you tomorrow," Ryan answered, briefly making eye contact. He turned and walked out of the room, and Kathryn sat back down at her desk.

She thought for a minute, and then decided that she was going to say something to his parents. His behavior was so different than it had been, and she figured that it was most likely something more serious than merely being tired. Kathryn opened her computer and pulled up the contact information that she had on file.

She noticed that Ryan did not have parents listed on his form, but instead he had a guardian named Carson Gregory. She shrugged her shoulders and started writing an email.

Dear Mr. Gregory,

Hello. My name is Kathryn Nichols and I am Ryan's Language Arts teacher. I am sending you this note because I am a bit concerned about Ryan. I noticed that today and yesterday he was much more withdrawn in class than he had been up to this point.

He is normally very talkative and contributes a lot to classroom discussions, but for the past two days he has not engaged at all. He is not disruptive or anything, but he just sits and looks off into the distance.

I talked with him a little bit after class today to let him know that I was concerned, but he told me that he was just tired. That may be what is going on, but I wanted to say something to you just in case there is something more serious that he is dealing with.

Please let me know if there is anything that I can do. I have really enjoyed getting to know Ryan. He is a very intelligent young man and has a lot of insight that he brings to the class.

Sincerely,
Kathryn Nichols

That evening Kathryn checked her email and was pleased to see that Mr. Gregory had responded.

Dear Ms. Nichols,

Thank you very much for your email. I really appreciate your concern, and it is nice to know that Ryan has someone looking out for him. I agree that he is a very intelligent young man, and I have always thought that he was wise beyond his years.

In regards to the change in his demeanor lately, I can explain what is happening. As you undoubtedly noticed in the contact information, I am Ryan's guardian and not his parent. I am actually his uncle. Sadly, Ryan's parents were killed in a car accident three years ago, and Ryan came to live with me.

Saturday is the anniversary of their death, so this is a particularly rough time for him. I will make sure that he stays on top of his assignments, but his classroom participation will be lower this week.

Thank you, again, for your concern.

Sincerely,
Carson Gregory

Kathryn finished reading the email and felt her eyes fill up with tears. She couldn't believe all that Ryan had to deal with. She pressed reply and wrote a brief response to Ryan's uncle.

Dear Mr. Gregory,

Thank you for your reply. I am so sorry for your loss. Please know that I will not discuss this with Ryan, unless he brings it up with me first.

Let me know if there is anything else I can do.

Sincerely,
Kathryn Nichols

The next day when Ryan walked into class he went and dropped a note on Kathryn's desk before finding his seat. Once the students were working on their assignments, Kathryn unfolded the note to see what it said. Her eyes filled with tears once again as she read the few short lines.

Dear Ms. Nichols,

My uncle told me you wrote him, and that he told you about my parents. Thanks for caring about me. You're a good teacher. This week is awful, but I will be okay.

Ryan

Kathryn looked over at Ryan and was surprised to see him looking at her. She smiled and he gave a small smile in return, and then looked back at his book. Kathryn knew that Ryan Gregory would be one of those students she would never forget.

Chapter 4 – Back to School Night

Kathryn sat in the break room at the school and smiled as she listened to the new teachers talk about how nervous they were for Back to School Night.

"I just don't know how to deal with parents," said Angela, a first year Spanish teacher. "I mean, I talk to students all day long, and I don't have any trouble doing that. But just the thought of having to talk to a room full of parents really scares me."

"I know what you mean," replied Marsha. "I'm even nervous, and I teach Public Speaking, for crying out loud! Are you nervous, Kathryn?"

"A little bit," Kathryn answered. "Adults can be intimidating. The good news, though, is that we only have each group of parents for ten minutes before they move on to the next class. That's not too tough."

The other two ladies nodded in agreement.

"You should have seen my last school," Kathryn said, laughing at the memory. "It was a small, private school. There were only about 50 students in each grade, and there were only two teachers for each subject. At back to school night they kept all of the parents together in the auditorium and then each teacher had to stand up and give their presentation in front of everyone in the room. It was a nightmare!"

"Seriously?" Marsha asked. "In front of everyone? All of the parents, the other teachers, and the administrators?"

"In front of everyone," Kathryn answered.

"Wow!" Angela responded. "There is no way that I would want to do that! I guess ten minutes at a time is a much better deal!"

"Yes, indeed," Kathryn said, gathering up her things to head back to her room. Kathryn smiled at the other two teachers. "Good luck tonight. You'll do great!"

Once she was back in her room, Kathryn went through her notes for the presentation she would give that evening. Kathryn liked the way that Back to School night was handled at this school. All of the parents would meet in the auditorium at the beginning of the night.

The principal would welcome everyone and give a few brief remarks and then dismiss the parents to go to their child's classes. The parents would spend ten minutes in each classroom, hearing from the teacher. Kathryn was happy to have the chance to give a presentation to each group, but also relieved that the time with them would be brief.

After school Kathryn went home to her apartment to change her clothes and freshen up. Although she wasn't as nervous as she had been at her old school, she still wanted to make a good impression on the parents.

Once back at the school, Kathryn checked to make sure her classroom was neat and orderly. She was in the middle of writing some notes on the board when she heard her door open. She looked over and was surprised to see Hodge standing in the doorway.

"Hello," she said. This was the first time she had spoken with him since he had asked her out, and she felt a bit awkward.

"Hey," he said. "I just wanted to see if you were ready for this tonight. It's your first Back to School night here at this school."

Kathryn smiled. "Oh. Well yeah, I guess I'm ready. It will be over before I know it."

Hodge laughed. "You're right. It will be. And I guess this isn't your first time doing this, is it? You've taught before. Just not here."

"Nope, not my first time," Kathryn answered. She felt herself relaxing and realized that there was something about Hodge that put her at ease. "Are you ready?" she asked.

"Oh yeah, I'm ready," he answered, a slight smirk forming on his face. "I thought that this year I might have the parents do some exercises, maybe shoot a few hoops."

Kathryn laughed. "That would make for a very memorable night!"

"I agree. Somehow I don't think the administration would be as amused," he said.

"Probably not," Kathryn answered.

Hodge walked over to the pile of papers that Kathryn had set out on a table. "What are these?" he asked, picking up one of the sheets and looking at it.

"Those are what I am handing out to the parents," she said. She walked over to him. "I outlined what we are going to be studying this year, the expectations that I have, and the specific dates that they should be aware of. It also has all of my contact information."

"That's very helpful," Hodge said. "I like that you have it all on one sheet. I send home about ten different papers over the course of the year and it just seems so wasteful. Can I take one of these to use as a template?"

"Sure," Kathryn said.

Hodge folded the paper and put it in his pocket. "Thanks," he said. "Can I tell you something without it getting weird and causing you to avoid me for another three weeks?"

"Hey! I haven't been avoiding you," Kathryn said

Hodge just looked down at her.

"Okay, fine. So maybe I have been avoiding you just a little bit," she admitted. "I just didn't know what to say to you."

"It's okay," he answered. "I totally get it. Anyway, can I say something to you?"

"Sure," Kathryn responded.

"You look absolutely beautiful tonight," Hodge said.

"Thank you," Kathryn said, looking down at the floor. She didn't know what else she should say. She appreciated the compliment and realized that she liked hearing it from him, but she also was sticking to her commitment to not date him.

"You're welcome," Hodge replied. "Okay, that's enough of that. I'm going to go get my stuff ready, and I'll let you get back to what you were doing. Have a great night!"

"Bye," Kathryn answered, still unsure of how to respond to his compliment. She watched him walk down the hallway, amazed at his confidence. She turned back to her room and, convinced that everything was exactly the way she wanted it, sat down to read a book and wait for the parents to arrive.

As Kathryn had suspected, the night went by quickly, and without incident. The parents were all very kind and respectful, and she was impressed with how many were actually there. Every class period was full, and she was delighted to see just how involved the parents were.

When Kathryn got home that evening she changed into her most comfortable pajamas and sat down read more of her book.

She tried to concentrate on the novel, but her mind kept going back to the events of the evening. She realized that as she was interacting with the adults who were there, she had been trying to figure out which one of the people she saw was Ryan's uncle, Carson Gregory.

Kathryn had been in touch with Carson three more times after their first emails. She had written him a quick note on the anniversary of Ryan's parents' death. Kathryn wanted to let Carson know that she was thinking of him and Ryan, and wanted him to let her know if there was anything she could do. Carson had responded that he was grateful for her thoughtfulness.

The following week Carson had written to see if Ryan was still distant, or if he was more talkative in class. Kathryn had responded that Ryan was fully engaged in class again and seemed to be doing well.

The last time that Kathryn had communicated with Carson was to let him know that Ryan had written a beautiful poem and that Kathryn had encouraged him to enter it into a writing contest. Carson responded that he had also loved the poem, and that he would follow up with Ryan.

Kathryn tried to picture all of the faces that she had seen, but she still didn't know which one was Carson, or if he had been there at all. She had thought about him so often, intrigued by the type of man who would take in his teenaged nephew.

She had looked on the contact information and found out that Carson was single. She didn't know if he had a girlfriend or not, but she knew that he definitely was not married. She felt strangely happy that he wasn't married, and was surprised to find that she cared so much.

Realizing that she was never going to be able to concentrate on her book, Kathryn decided to check her email one last time before watching some television. As she opened her email she got the answer to at least one question – Carson had been there that evening. She still didn't know what he looked like, but he had been there. Kathryn smiled as she read his message.

Hello Kathryn,

Thank you for hosting all of us at Back to School Night tonight. I appreciate all of the information that you gave, and I can tell that it is going to be a great year. I can also see why Ryan likes your class so much.

At the risk of seeming too forward, I would also like to tell you that you are an absolutely beautiful woman. I was wondering if you would like to join me for coffee some evening so we can continue this conversation and keep getting to know each other better, but in person.

Let me know what you think,

Carson

Kathryn looked at the email for a minute, not knowing how she should respond. Although she had enjoyed the email correspondence with Carson, and she appreciated his kind words, she didn't know if she wanted to agree to a date with him.

On the other hand, she was really intrigued by him and felt that a man who would willingly take in a teenager was the exact type of man that she wanted to get to know.

After staring at her screen for another five minutes, Kathryn decided that she would sleep on it and make her decision in the morning.
She shut her computer and got ready for bed, contemplating what she would do.

Chapter 5 – Two Offers

The next morning Kathryn woke up and knew what her response would be. It wasn't necessarily the response that she wanted to send, but she knew that it was the response that she should send. After pouring herself a cup of coffee, she sat down to her computer and began to type.

Hello Carson,

Thank you for your note, and thank you for coming to Back to School Night. I think it is wonderful that you are so involved in Ryan's education. I know that your support is one of the reasons that he is such a good student.

To answer your question, I appreciate your kind words and the offer of coffee, but right now I cannot accept. You are the guardian for one of my students, and I just think it would make things a bit complicated. I wouldn't want Ryan to feel uncomfortable, and I wouldn't want to make things awkward with the rest of the students either.

That being said, I have really enjoyed our communication to this point. I would like to get to know you better. Would you be willing to continue with the just the emails for a little while longer before we get that coffee you mentioned?

Let me know,

Kathryn

Kathryn got ready for work, curious to know what Carson's response would be. No matter what he said, she knew that she had made the right decision. Kathryn had always tried to keep her personal life separate from her work life, and as much as she felt drawn to Carson, she knew that she needed to be responsible. Dating the uncle and guardian of her students, especially so early in the school year, would open up the potential for a lot of problems.

Kathryn wasn't able to check her email until her morning break, but she felt her heart skip a beat when she saw that Carson had replied.

Good morning, Kathryn.

Let's keep this conversation going. I respect your decision to hold off on the coffee for a bit, and it makes sense. But I most definitely want to get to know you better.

So, tell me, Ms. Nichols, want made you want to be a Language Arts teacher?

Carson

"Well you look happy. Are you having a good day?"

The sound of Hodge's deep voice startled Kathryn. She quickly closed out her email and blushed as she looked up at him.

"You can say that," she answered. "Good morning."

"Good morning," Hodge replied. "I am sorry if I startled you. I just wanted to stop by and see how things went last night. I came by your room after the evening was over, but you had already gone home."

"Oh, yeah. I was ready to get home. It was a good night, though. I actually had a lot of fun," Kathryn said. "What about you? Did you put the adults through a workout?"

Hodge smiled and shook his head. "No, not this year. Maybe I will after I pass my tenth anniversary here at this school. It will be my fun way of celebrating!"

Kathryn laughed. "How long have you been here?"

"Eight years," Hodge replied. "I came hear my first year out of college and I haven't left."

"Wow," Kathryn said. "That's impressive. I don't blame you, though. This is a great school."

"It really is," Hodge agreed, sitting on the edge of one of the desks. "Plus, I get to coach all three of my favorite sports. I really couldn't ask for much more than that."

"You coach three sports?" Kathryn asked. "Let me guess. I know football is the first one. I am going to guess basketball and baseball for the other two."

"Very good," Hodge said.

"Thank you." Kathryn looked at the clock. "I don't want to rush you out of here, but I only have ten more minutes until my next class starts, and I need to get some more coffee first."

"Oh, I understand," Hodge said, standing up. "Coffee is a must!"

Kathryn nodded. "Absolutely!"

Hodge turned started to leave and then turned around one more time. "Speaking of coffee, do you still think it would be unwise to get some coffee with me after school some evening?"

Kathryn could not deny that she was attracted to Hodge. He was gorgeous, and she enjoyed talking with him, but as she considered his offer she thought of her emails with Carson.

"Yes," she said, smiling. "I still believe that right now it would be unwise to get some coffee with you after school some evening."

"Just checking," Hodge said. "Have a great day, Ms. Nichols."

"You too, Mr. Hodges."

Kathryn walked towards the break room, shaking her head at the fact she had turned down two dates in the past two days.

When it rains, it pours, she thought. At least it's not boring.

Chapter 6 - Emails

Kathryn settled onto her couch and opened her computer, eager to see what Carson had to say. For the past month they had been emailing several times every day and she always looked forward to hearing from him.

Hello Kathryn,

I wanted to let you know that I saw you at the football game tonight. You looked like you were having fun, although you looked cold.

I have noticed the way that you always seem to be with the younger teachers. Are you some sort of mentor to them?

Carson

Kathryn rubbed her hands together, remembering how cold she had been earlier in the evening.

Hi Carson,

You saw me at the game? I didn't see you, obviously. I don't know what you look like. I even talked to Ryan a bit at the game. Were you sitting near him? I think it's fun that you go to the games, even though Ryan doesn't play.

I know that he's a golfer. Do you go to his golf tournaments, too? He told me that all of his tournaments are out of town, which makes it difficult for people to come and watch him. I am not a mentor to the new teachers. I am just their friend. I remember what it was like my first year, and I want to make sure that they know they aren't alone.

I was very cold tonight, and I still haven't fully warmed up!

Kathryn

Kathryn went and took a shower. She knew that the shower would warm her up, but she also didn't want to be the type of person who sat and stared at her inbox, waiting for an email to appear. Once she was out of the shower and in her pajamas, she opened her computer again.

Hey Kathryn,

I hope you get warm! It was so chilly tonight. You should probably dress warmer for the rest of the games. It's only going to get colder as the season goes on.

I was not sitting with Ryan at the game. He does his thing and I do mine. I keep an eye on him, but not too close. I don't want to cramp his style.

I go to Ryan's tournaments when I can, but sometimes they interfere with my work schedule. He's a good golfer.

He has been playing since he was a little boy. Ryan used to golf with his dad, so when his dad died he thought about quitting. After six months or so he decided that he would still play, and he dedicates every tournament to his father's memory. It's a beautiful thing to watch. He's a great kid.

I think it's cool that you are doing that for the new teachers. You'll probably help them a lot. From what Ryan tells me, you are the best teacher ever.

Carson

Kathryn smiled. She sensed that Ryan had a bit of a crush on her, but she knew that it was nothing serious. Kathryn loved the way that Carson talked about Ryan. She could tell that he was really proud of his nephew, and she thought that it was really sweet.

Hi Carson,

I wouldn't say that I'm the best teacher ever, but I do love my job.

Speaking of my job, I just realized that I don't know what you do for work. You have never told me! Why not? Are you a secret agent? Are you trying to hide something? Maybe it's just never come up…

Kathryn

Kathryn realized that it was close to midnight. She decided to go to bed, but she knew that she would check her email first thing in the morning. As soon as she woke up, before she had even had a cup of coffee, she was looking at her computer screen.

Hello Kathryn,

You are right. We have never discussed my career.

It's not that I have anything to hide; it's just that we have talked about so many other things that it never came up.

You know that I'm 30 years old, that I have lived in the same community for most of my life, and that I love jazz music.

You also know that I love sports. Well, I have been fortunate enough to take that love of sports and turn it into a career. I work with youth, coaching them in many different athletics. I have been working in this field ever since I was 14 and started volunteering with the local recreation department. So, that leads me to my next question. You mentioned that you are not that fond of sports, or of athletes especially. Can I ask why?

Carson

Kathryn sighed and closed her computer. She wasn't surprised to find out that Carson worked with youth. He cared so deeply for his nephew, and throughout their conversations he had always shown a lot of insight into the teenage mindset. However, she was very surprised to find out that he was an athlete. She knew that he loved to watch professional and college sports, but he had never mentioned playing or coaching.

Kathryn quickly opened her computer again, deciding to write him back before she lost her nerve.

Dear Carson,

I am sure that you are an excellent coach. You know so much about teenagers and undoubtedly have a huge impact on their lives.

To clear things up, it's not that I don't enjoy sports. I like watching football and baseball. I love to play softball and tennis, and I also enjoy hiking and skiing. My issue with sports actually comes down to one sport in particular: basketball.

To be perfectly honest, my issue with basketball has nothing to do with basketball. It has to do with basketball players. More specifically, it has to do with two basketball players.

When I was in high school, I dated a boy who was on the basketball team. He was very good and went on to play in college. He was a year older than me, and when he graduated he decided that he didn't want to be tied down when he went off to school. The problem was, he didn't bother to tell me. He simply stopped communicating with me. He didn't call or write, and I heard nothing from him until he came home for Winter Break and brought his new girlfriend with him.

He was my first love, and he broke my heart. After that, every time I went to a basketball game I was reminded of him, so I chose to avoid the games instead.

After that happened it took me a few years before I was willing to date again. It wasn't until my senior year of college that I actually got into another relationship. He was also a basketball player. We dated for nearly a year until I came home and found out he had been cheating on me, with my roommate. I haven't really dated – or enjoyed a basketball game – since then.

So there you have it - the full story of why I avoid athletes. I know that it was a long time ago and I am ready to move on, but the memories are still painful.

Okay, now that I have told you my dating history... what's yours?

Kathryn

Kathryn spent the rest of the day grading papers. She enjoyed reading the things that her students wrote, and she was pleased to see that they were all becoming strong writers. After a couple of hours Kathryn looked to see if Carson responded to her message, and she was not disappointed.

Hello Kathryn,

Thank you for being honest with me, and I am sorry that you had to go through that hurt when you were younger.

My dating story is pretty boring. I had a couple of girlfriends when I was in high school, but nothing too serious. I dated quite a bit when I was in college, but I never settled down with anyone.

I just never found anyone who really inspired me, or who understood my love for working with young people. Once I graduated college, I started working.

I was very focused on building my career, and although I went out on dates every so often, I didn't feel like I had the time to put into a relationship.

Then, three years ago, Ryan's parents passed away. He came to live with me, and my entire life changed. I have not been out on a date since then.

Now, I am having a nice time emailing a beautiful woman, one whom I hope to hang out with in person soon. No pressure, though. I will wait as long as you like.

Carson

Kathryn smiled and immediately began typing her response.

Carson,

I don't think your dating history is boring. I think it shows that you are committed to your nephew and your career, and that you take relationships seriously. I think that is very admirable.

As far as hanging out in person goes, I just looked at the calendar and realized that we will be doing that very soon. Parent-Teacher Conferences are coming up in two weeks, so I will be setting appointments with everyone. We will see each other then.

I must admit I am looking forward to it.

Kathryn

Kathryn went out for dinner with a few of her friends. When she got home she decided to check her email one last time before going to bed.

Hey Kathryn,

Parent-Teacher Conferences, huh? Well okay. I wouldn't exactly call that a date, but at least we will be able to talk face to face.

I am looking forward to it, but I am also a bit nervous.

Until then, let's keep up the emails.

Carson

As Kathryn fell asleep that night she realized that she had never looked forward to Parent-Teacher Conferences as much as she was looking forward them this year. She was ready to finally meet Carson in person.

Chapter 7 – The Conference

Kathryn looked in the mirror one last time, making sure that she looked her absolute best.

She had four conferences scheduled for that afternoon, but the one that she was the most excited for was the very last one, scheduled for 6:00.

She tried to put Carson out of her mind as she met with the other parents. A lot of teachers were often uncomfortable with conferences, but Kathryn really enjoyed them. She liked being able to talk directly with parents about their child. She felt that it helped her get a better understanding of her students, which in turn made her a better teacher.

After the third meeting, Kathryn went to the bathroom one last time. She ran a brush through her hair and straightened her clothes.

Here we go, she thought. It's time to meet him.

At 6:00 sharp the classroom door opened and Kathryn eagerly looked to see who was there.

She felt a twinge of disappointment when she saw Hodge standing in the doorway, smiling at her.

"Oh, hey Hodge," she said, trying to sound friendly.

"Hey," he said. "You seem distracted. Is everything okay?"

"Yeah, everything is fine," she said. "I'm just waiting for my next conference to start. It is scheduled for 6:00, so I don't really have time to talk."

Kathryn walked to her desk, hoping that Hodge would take the hint and leave. It wasn't that she didn't enjoy being around Hodge. Over the past few months they had actually formed a fun friendship, and normally she was happy when he stopped by her room. Tonight, though, Carson was the only person she wanted to see.

Rather than leave, Hodge sat down in one of the chairs.

Kathryn shook her head. "Seriously, Hodge, I am expecting someone any minute. It would be awkward if you are here."

Hodge cleared his throat. "Oh, well, um, yeah. I have a conference tonight."

"Yeah? I didn't realize that kids had conferences for PE." Kathryn said, looking at the clock again. "What time is your meeting?"

"6:00."

"Well, it is 6:00 now," Kathryn said, smiling. She walked over and opened her door. "You don't want to be late."

"I know," Hodge said. He cleared his throat again, smiling nervously. "My conference isn't about PE. It's actually with another teacher."

"Oh?" Kathryn asked, confused.

"Yeah," Hodge answered. "With my nephew's teacher, to be precise."

Kathryn stared at Hodge. "What? What do you mean?"

"Kathryn, I'm Ryan's uncle," Hodge said softly.

Kathryn stared at him for a minute and then shook her head in disbelief. "You're Carson?"

"Yes."

"You're Carson Gregory? I don't understand. Isn't your last name Hodges?"

Hodge nodded. "Yes. My full name is Carson Gregory-Hodges."

Kathryn walked over and sat down at her desk. "Okay..." she said, slowly letting out her breath. She looked at Hodge.

Hodge took a deep breath and continued. "Ryan's father, Jason, was my older brother. He was a very successful athlete and had a great reputation in school. All of the teachers loved him and it seemed like sports journalists were writing about him every day. When I got into high school I wanted to make sure that anything that I accomplished was based on my own merit and not on the fact that I was Jason's brother. I decided that the best way to do that was to have a different last name, so I dropped the Gregory and just went by Hodges. That soon became Hodge, and it stuck."

Kathryn looked over at Hodge, trying to process all that she was hearing.

Hodge continued with his explanation. "When Ryan came to live with me, I decided that for school stuff it would be easiest if he and I had the same last name. It made the paperwork easier, and it was a simple way that I could honor my brother's memory."

Hodges eyes filled with tears and he was quite for a few minutes before he continued. "Ryan had been through so much already, I wanted to make it as easy as possible for him. So I just used that last name and figured it wouldn't make that much of a difference."

Kathryn nodded. "That all makes sense," she said. "But why didn't you just tell me from the very beginning? Why did you feel the need to hide it from me?"

Hodge put his head down. "I'm sorry that I didn't tell you. I know I should have told you from the beginning. It's just that I really wanted a chance to get to know you, but you seemed to push me away every time I tried to talk with you."

Kathryn grabbed Ryan's file and walked over and sat across from Hodge.

"Okay," she said. "I don't really know what to do with this. But I do know that you are here for a conference about Ryan, so we should get to that."

"Really?" Hodge asked. "We aren't going to talk about this?"

"Carson – or Hodge – I don't really know what to say right now. I feel like you tricked me, and I really don't like being tricked," Kathryn said, her voice trembling.
"I was honest with you. I told you personal things. I feel kind of foolish, not knowing who you really were."

Hodge nodded and looked into Kathryn's eyes. "I am so sorry for that. You shouldn't feel foolish. I have truly enjoyed emailing you all of this time. I feel like you have gotten to know the real me. Here at school it's different. I'm different. I almost feel like Carson and Hodge are two completely different people. Do you understand?"

Kathryn nodded. "I do understand. And I would have understood if you told me the truth from the very beginning."

Hodge sighed. "I'm not sure you would have, Kathryn. You pushed me away. You never gave me a chance. I noticed that the very first day that I met you at orientation. I tried to talk to you. I tried to get to know you, and you shut me down. Do you remember that?"

Kathryn nodded.

"Then after that, I asked you out. I asked if you would get some coffee, and you said you didn't think it would be wise. And I understand that you want to be careful, but I just wanted a chance to talk to you outside of school. I wanted you to get to know me away from all of this." Hodge pointed to the classroom.

"But then you emailed me about Ryan. I noticed that you were different in your emails. You were more open, and more willing to chat. So I took you up on the opportunity. I figured that once you got to know me, the real me, you would see that I'm not someone that you need to avoid."

Kathryn looked at Hodge, trying to figure out what she was feeling and what she should say. Finally she shrugged her shoulders. "Hodge, we're not going to get this worked out tonight. To be honest, I don't even know what I am feeling. I just feel confused. Let's just put everything else aside and talk about Ryan."

Hodge nodded. "Okay," he said. "I can do that."

"Great," Kathryn said. She opened Ryan's file and the two of them spent the next half hour talking about Ryan. Kathryn showed Hodge some of Ryan's best work, and they discussed how much he had already learned since school began.

"Well, Ryan absolutely loves your class," Hodge said. "Last week he had a really bad cold. I told him he could stay home from school but he said that he didn't want to miss your class. He said something about comparing and contrasting the Bronte sisters or something."

Kathryn smiled. "That's great," she said. "I am so happy that he enjoys my class as much as he does. He really seems to have a good understanding of everything. As far as comparing and contrasting the sisters, he did a great job! I wish all of my students were as dedicated as he is."

Hodge smiled. "From what I hear, It's not just Ryan everyone loves your class. All of my students talk about you. The ones who don't have you for a teacher this semester said that they are going to try and switch into your class!"

Kathryn laughed. "You're exaggerating!"

"I'm not," Hodge insisted. "People are drawn to you, Kathryn. You're an incredible teacher. You're an incredible person, actually."

Kathryn didn't say anything. She looked into Hodge's eyes and felt pulse quicken.

After a minute, Hodge leaned back in his seat. "So is there anything else?"

Kathryn shook her head. "Not that I can think of."

Kathryn and Hodge sat and looked at each other, neither one speaking. Finally Hodge leaned forward and said quietly, "I really am sorry."

Kathryn nodded. "I know you are. And you are right. I did push you away in person."

Hodge smiled. "I know. And I understand why you did. I remember what you told me about the basketball players that broke your heart. And here I am, everything about me indicating that I am a basketball player, trying to get your attention. But Kathryn, I want you to hear me on this. If you trust me with your heart, I won't break it."

Kathryn looked down at her hands. "I just don't know what to say now. Or what to do."

Hodge took a deep breath. "I have an idea," he said. "I know that you need time to process things, so why don't you take a few days to think things over. I won't bother you here at school, or email you. At 7:00 on Saturday night, I will be sitting at Davey's Coffee Shop on 3rd Street. If you are willing to come and have coffee with me and see where we go from here, meet me there at 7:00. If you don't want to move forward, then don't come. Does that sound fair?"

Kathryn thought about it for a minute. "Yes, that sounds like a good plan."

"Okay, good," Hodge said. He stood up and walked to the doorway. "I hope to see you Saturday night, Kathryn. But if not, I will understand. If you can't meet me, send me an email and let me know what you want. If you want to keep emailing, I will do that. If you want me to leave you alone for good, I will do that. I will respect what you decide. And again, I'm sorry I didn't tell you everything from the start."

Kathryn watched him walk out of the room then sat back down in her chair. Tears rolled down her cheeks as she tried to understand everything that she was feeling. Part of her was still angry that Hodge had tricked her, but deep down she understood why he had done it that way. She knew that she never would have given him a chance.

Kathryn dried her tears and gathered her things to go home. Once she was home, she sat down on her couch and truly examined her heart. She thought of how much she had enjoyed the emails with Carson and how comfortable she felt sharing her thoughts and feelings with him.

She also thought about Hodge, and how attractive he was. She remembered the electricity she felt whenever he looked at her, and how she felt completely drawn to him.

When Kathryn realized that both of these men were, in fact, the same person, her heart started to pound. She knew that he had all of the traits that she was looking for in a partner. He was kind and compassionate. Kathryn felt a surge of emotion as she thought about the way that Hodge had taken in Ryan.

He was 27 years old, she thought. 27 years old, handsome, and successful. Here he was, pretty much able to do whatever he wanted. Then a horrible tragedy struck, and he stepped up. He took in his nephew, no questions asked.

This was the type of man that she could love. This was the type of man that she suspected she already did love.

Kathryn fell asleep that night with a smile on her face, eagerly awaiting Saturday night.

Chapter 8 – Coffee at Last

Kathryn sat in her car, working up the nerve to walk into the coffee shop. She knew that once she went in there, everything would change. She knew that the feelings that she had for Carson Hodges were deeper than anything she had ever felt.

Although she knew that this meant there was the possibility that she would get hurt, she also knew that there was a the possibility that she would be happier than she ever thought possible.

Kathryn got out of the car and walked to the door, nervously checking her appearance in the window. She looked inside and saw Hodge sitting at a table, quietly reading a book.

Man, he looks good, she thought. He was wearing a nice shirt and jeans, and Kathryn realized that she had never seen him in anything other than sports gear.

As Kathryn watched Hodge, she thought about Ryan. She wondered what this would mean for him, and wondered if it was fair to him. Was he ready for his uncle to date someone? Would Ryan be okay with the fact that his teacher was his uncle's girlfriend? As Kathryn thought about Ryan, she remembered all of the interactions they had had in class. She knew that he liked and respected her, and she knew that he trusted his Uncle. Kathryn knew that whatever happened, Ryan would be okay.

Kathryn opened the door and Hodge looked up and made eye contact her. A slow smile spread across his face as he stood up and walked towards her. Kathryn stood where she was, her heart racing. She loved this man, and knew that she wanted to spend the rest of her life with him.

Hodge stood in front of her and smiled down at her. He put his arms around her and pulled her close to him. She tipped her face up towards him and he leaned down and covered her mouth with his. Kathryn surrendered to his kiss, fully knowing that everything would be just fine.

When Hodge pulled back, his brown eyes were glistening with tears. "Hello," he said, his voice husky with emotion.

"Hello," Kathryn said softly.

"I'm so glad you came," Hodge said.

"Me too," Kathryn answered.

"Can I tell you something?" Hodge asked.

"Yes."
Hodge leaned down and put his lips next to Kathryn's ear. "I love you," he whispered.

"I love you, too," Kathryn replied.

Hodge kissed Kathryn again, and then they sat down and finally had a cup of coffee. As they drank coffee and talked, Hodge told Kathryn how excited Ryan was for them.

"He knew about this," Kathryn asked.

"Well, he knew about the possibility of this," Hodge responded. "He told me that he really hoped that you showed. He also said that if you truly believed everything that you said about love and romance, then you would be here."

Kathryn laughed. "He really said that?" Kathryn asked.

"Yep!" Hodge said.

Kathryn reached over and put her hand in Hodge's.

"He's a smart kid," she said, softly.

"That he is," Hodge agreed. "That he is."

Six months later, Kathryn and Hodge were married. They had a simple ceremony on the beach, and Ryan served as the best man.

I write under the pseudonym: Urquhart Randolph. I like to write great romance stories that take you on a blazing journey - tears, laughter (may be both) or just a steamy hot fun (perhaps all of them).

Please... leave a review, regardless if you think my book deserves 1* or 5 * let me know if you had enjoyed this great story?

THANK YOU ☺

subscribe
VISIT US
Enroll in our VIP list.
Be the first to be notified on our latest published book.
Downloading for free gifts.